A Lift-the-Flap Book

Great Easter Egg Hunt

Suzy-Jane Tanner

First published in the United Kingdom in 1999 by David Bennett Books Limited, United Kingdom. Reprinted in 1999.

BRITISH LIBRARY CATALOGUING-IN-PUBLICATION DATA: A catalogue record for this book is available from the British Library.
ISBN 1 85602 285 4
Manufactured in China.

Hooray!
It’s Easter Day!

It's time for the great Easter egg hunt.

Let's look in the kitchen dresser first.

What's in the cupboard?

Are there any Easter eggs under the stairs?

Perhaps the eggs are under the quilt.

Let's search in the playhouse.

Are the eggs
in the flowerbed?

No one knows
where the eggs can be.

But what is in this basket?

Happy Easter, everyone!

The End